Copyright © 2003 by Atlantis, an imprint of Orell Füssli Verlag AG Zürich, Switzerland
First published in Switzerland under the title *Stomatenpaghetti.*
English translation copyright © 2005 by North-South Books Inc., New York

First published in the United States, Great Britain, Canada, Australia, and New Zealand in 2005
by North-South Books, an imprint of NordSüd Verlag AG, Gossau Zürich, Switzerland.
Distributed in the United States by North-South Books Inc., New York.

Library of Congress Cataloging-in-Publication Data is available.
A CIP catalogue record for this book is available from The British Library.
ISBN 0-7358-1991-2 (trade edition)
1 3 5 7 9 10 8 6 4 2
ISBN 0-7358-1992-0 (library edition)
1 3 5 7 9 10 8 6 4 2
Printed in Belgium

For more information about our books, and the authors and artists
who create them, visit our web site: www.northsouth.com

Susanne Vettiger

Basghetti

Spaghetti

Illustrated by Marie-Anne Räber

NORTH-SOUTH BOOKS / NEW YORK / LONDON

Oscar the little crab was on his way to school. As he scuttled along he sang a song that he'd made up about spaghetti, the food he loved best in the world.

Oh, I love, love, love spaghetti.
It's scrumptious and delicious,
And really so nutritious.
That's why I'm always ready,
To gobble up spaghetti.
Yum, yum, yum, yum, yum!

Oscar had once tried to teach his classmates the rhyme, but Oscar had a problem. Whenever he was nervous or excited or frightened, his tongue got all twisted and he jumbled up his words. So when he recited the rhyme in front of the class, it came out:

Oh, I love, love, love basghetti,
It's spumtrious and ledicious,
And really so nunitious.
That's why I'm awlays dready,
To boggle up basghetti,
Yum, yum, yum, yum, yum!

How the other students had laughed!

This morning, as Oscar scurried across the green reef, a shark popped up in front of him. The shark was huge, with sharp, scary teeth. Oscar was terrified. He hid behind a sea urchin, peeking out now and then. After a while, the shark swam away, and Oscar, all six legs trembling, hurried as fast as he could to school.

His teacher, Mrs. Pembleton, was waiting for him. "You're late, Oscar," she said.

Oscar was so excited that he started sputtering, jumbling everything up.

"Sorry, Mrs. Meppleman . . . I mean Mrs. Pepperton, I mean . . . well there was a fremotious snark. . . . it was gigantimous . . . and I hid behind a sea munchkin . . . and . . ."

All the students started laughing at him. Mrs. Pembleton just shook her head.

No one believes me, Oscar thought sadly. He was so upset that he ran away.

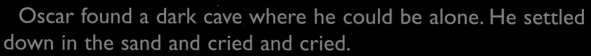

Oscar found a dark cave where he could be alone. He settled down in the sand and cried and cried.

Right next to Oscar lay Susie the sweeper fish. She was sound asleep. She'd been busy all night cleaning—vacuuming up the ocean floor, dusting off the reefs, pruning the sea grass. Susie rolled over. Her feelers brushed against something strange. It was Oscar.

"Hello there. I'm Susie. Who are you and why are you crying?" she asked.

"I'm Oscar," he replied. And then he told Susie all about the shark and how he jumbled everything up and the others laughed at him. "I just wish I could talk right," he said with a sigh.

"Come with me," said Susie. "I know someone who can help you."

Susie carried Oscar on her back. They crossed the coral reef and there on the other side, dark and majestic, lay a sunken ship. Oscar stared, amazed. There was a sign on the ship:
DOCTOR OCTOPUS, SPEECH FIXER.

The octopus came right out to greet his visitors.
"This is my friend Oscar. He has a small problem. Maybe
you can help him," said Susie. She made an elegant swoop
in the water, and said good-bye to both of them.

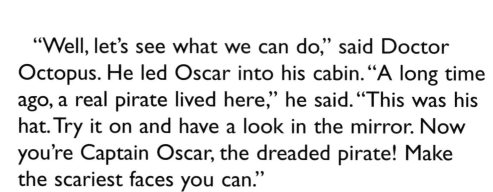

"Well, let's see what we can do," said Doctor Octopus. He led Oscar into his cabin. "A long time ago, a real pirate lived here," he said. "This was his hat. Try it on and have a look in the mirror. Now you're Captain Oscar, the dreaded pirate! Make the scariest faces you can."

A little shy at first, then braver and braver, Oscar made faces—horrible faces. This is great! he thought. I feel like a bold buccaneer. If only his classmates could see him now!

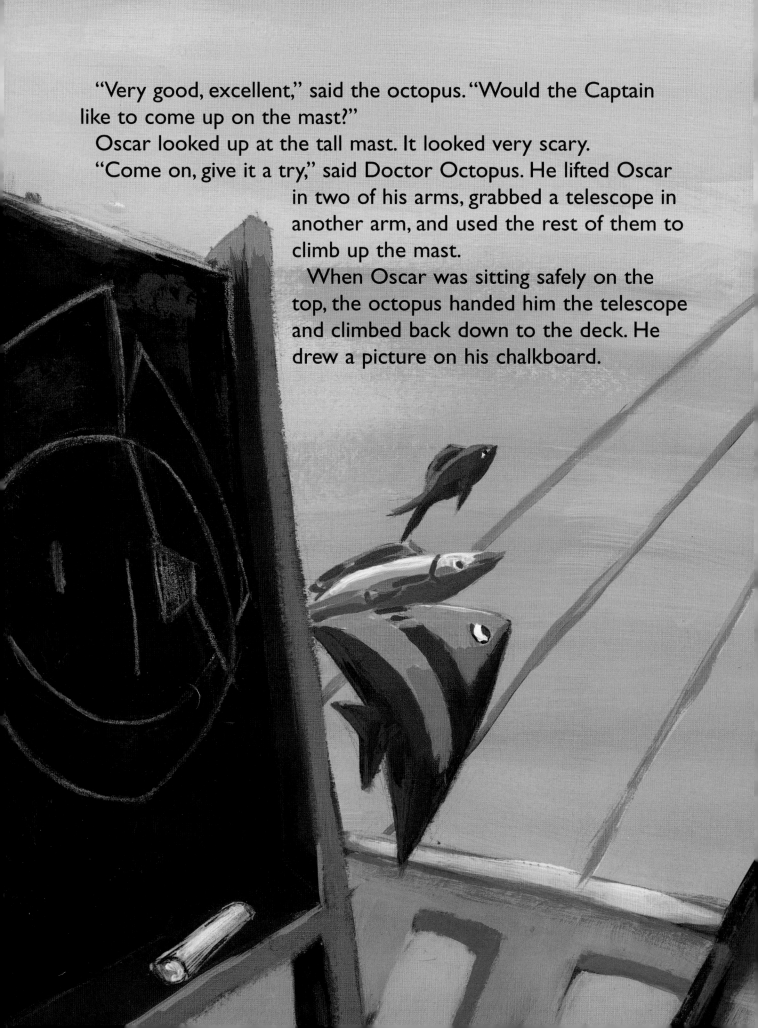

"Very good, excellent," said the octopus. "Would the Captain like to come up on the mast?"

Oscar looked up at the tall mast. It looked very scary.

"Come on, give it a try," said Doctor Octopus. He lifted Oscar in two of his arms, grabbed a telescope in another arm, and used the rest of them to climb up the mast.

When Oscar was sitting safely on the top, the octopus handed him the telescope and climbed back down to the deck. He drew a picture on his chalkboard.

"Tell me what this is!" he called to Oscar.

Oscar was trembling. He was so high up. Nervously he replied, "Fife reserver."

"Not bad," said the octopus. "Take a breath and try again, slowly this time."

"Rife leserver," said Oscar quietly. "I'll never be able to do it."

"Yes, you will, Oscar!" declared Doctor Octopus. "Try singing it—and pat your neck at the same time."

Oscar started to hum. He patted his neck and sang out, "Life preserver!"

"Good job, Oscar! Keep going," said the octopus. He drew another picture. "Try this one!"

Oscar kept singing and patting his neck. "Life preserver, life preserver, shark!" he sang out loud and clear. "I did it!"

"Bravo, Oscar!" cheered Doctor Octopus. He scampered up the mast and carried Oscar back to the deck.

There sat a little cannon. The octopus explained a new game to Oscar. "Whenever you say a tongue twister correctly, you get to fire off the cannon and try to knock over the cans."

It was difficult at first, but before long Oscar was reciting really hard ones like, "Peter Piper picked a peck of pickled peppers" and "She sells seashells by the seashore," without making a single mistake! He loved shooting off the cannon—and he managed to knock over lots of cans.

"That was great! What should we play next?" asked Oscar eagerly.

The octopus winked. "Let's look for pirate treasure!"

They hunted all over the ship. Finally Oscar found a big black box. Inside were hundreds of golden letters, filled with chocolate.

"Take as many as you want. You've earned them!" said Doctor Octopus.

Weeks went by. Oscar visited Doctor Octopus every day. He knew lots of good games, and Oscar did so well that even when he was nervous his words all came out perfectly! And every day he was rewarded with more golden letters.

Finally, Oscar was ready to go back to school. His teacher was glad to see him, and to celebrate his return, she made spaghetti for everyone.

It was a great spaghetti party. At the end, everyone sang Oscar's spaghetti song. Even Oscar, and this time he sang every word correctly—except for basghetti!

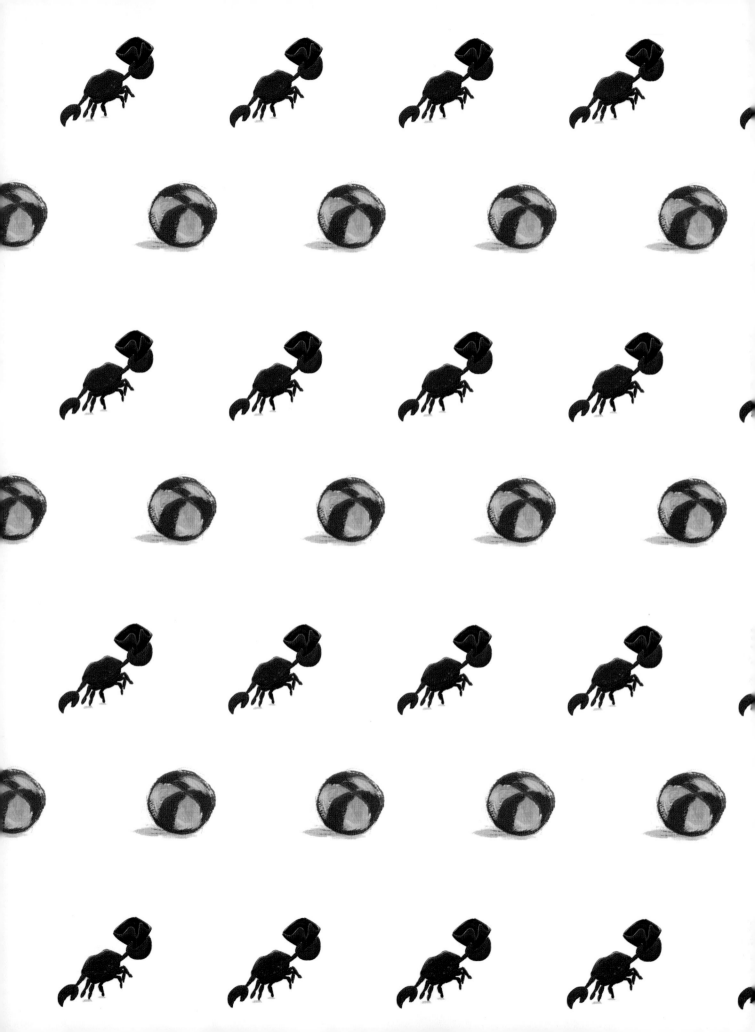

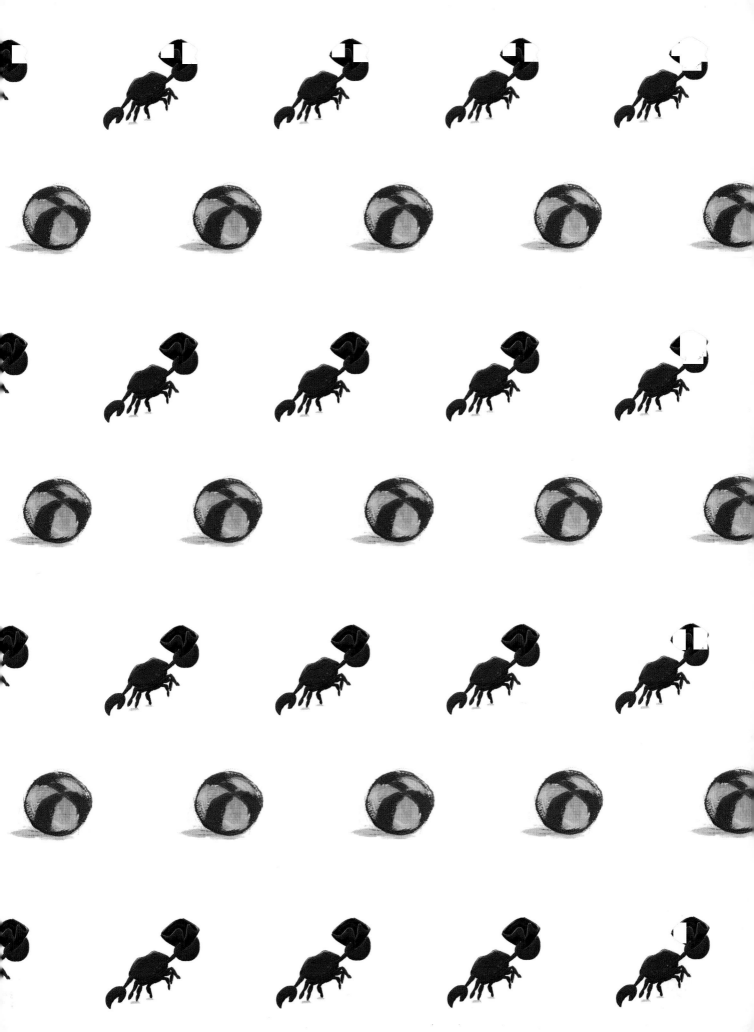